The Hit and Run
GANG ④
THE STREAK

Don't Miss Any of the
On-the-Field Excitement with
THE HIT AND RUN GANG
by Steven Kroll
from Avon Books

STEVEN KROLL grew up in New York City, where he was a pretty good first baseman and #3 hitter on baseball teams in Riverside Park. He graduated from Harvard University, spent almost seven years as an editor in book publishing, and then became a full-time writer. He is the author of more than fifty books for young people. He and his wife Abigail live in New York City and root for the Mets.

The Hit and Run GANG ④ THE STREAK

STEVEN KROLL

Illustrated by Meredith Johnson

AN AVON CAMELOT BOOK

THE HIT AND RUN GANG #4: THE STREAK is an original publication
of Avon Books. This work has never before appeared in book form.

AVON BOOKS
A division of
The Hearst Corporation
1350 Avenue of the Americas
New York, New York 10019

Copyright © 1992 by Steven Kroll
Illustrations copyright © 1992 by Avon Books
Published by arrangement with the author
Library of Congress Catalog Card Number: 91-92426
ISBN: 0-380-76410-5
RL: 2.8

First Avon Camelot Printing: July 1992

CAMELOT TRADEMARK REG. U.S. PAT. OFF. AND IN OTHER COUNTRIES, MARCA
REGISTRADA, HECHO EN U.S.A.

Printed in the U.S.A.

OPM   10   9   8   7   6   5   4   3   2   1

For Ingrid and Ned Beach

Contents

Contents

1. Keep It Alive!

"Brian Krause, shortstop."

Brian stepped into the batter's box. The slick-fielding, clutch-hitting shortstop of the Raymondtown Rockets anchored his back foot, took a few practice swings, got his arms back and ready, faced the pitcher for the Bradford Wildcats.

It was the top of the sixth. Two out and two on. The Rockets ahead 8–6 but needing another insurance run to protect their shaky lead.

Playing at home, the Wildcats had scored four of their six runs in the bottom of the fifth. The first three were against Andy McClellan, the Rockets' fireballing right-hander. Two walks, a one-out single up the middle, a wild pitch, a triple down the left field line, and Andy was headed for the showers. Justin Carr came in in relief, but on Justin's very first pitch, Matt Tully, the Wildcat first baseman, blasted a line drive right back to the mound.

Justin reached up his glove but only in time to deflect the ball off to his right. Phil Hubbard swooped down on it from third, grabbed it bare-handed, and pegged a strike to Luke Emory at the plate. But the Wildcat runner on third was quick as they come. He raced down the line so fast, he crossed home plate before Phil's throw thwacked into Luke's catcher's mitt.

Fortunately nothing ever seemed to rattle Justin. He came right back and struck out the next Wildcat hitter, then coaxed a slow ground ball to Vicky Lopez at second to end the inning. But the momentum seemed to be shifting, the hometown crowd was cheering, and the Wildcats were hot! Everyone knew it would be tough for Justin to hold them in the bottom of the sixth.

Now the Rockets were down to their last out. Back-to-back singles had put Luke on third and Phil on first. Could Brian drive them in?

Odds were that he could. Brian was short and chunky. He had red hair and glasses and a smudge of dirt always somewhere on his face. He didn't look as if he'd be much of a hitter, but he was.

He batted fifth in the order. He could hit for power or spray line drives to all fields. His secret was a low crouch that narrowed his strike zone, terrific bat speed, a short stroke, and tremendous anticipation. He *knew* where pitches were going to be before they got there. A right-handed hitter, he did almost equally well against righties and lefties. Best of all, he hardly ever struck out.

As Brian stood in and waited for the first pitch, anyone could see how focused he was. He didn't just want to drive in those extra runs. His ten-game hitting streak was on the line!

Somehow he'd messed up his earlier at bats. He'd grounded out, then lined out twice while his teammates were racking up their eight runs. It was frustrating not to be a part of that and more frustrating to think his streak might be slipping away.

It went back to the Rockets' first away game of the season. They were playing the Pelicans in Healesville, and Brian doubled to the left field corner, scoring Phil and igniting a late-inning rally that only just fell short. He'd gone on hitting through games against the Bombers, the Hurricanes, the Panthers, and the Jugglers. His bat seemed part of him, his swing so grooved and natural he could time it just right. Until now.

"Come on, Brian!" he heard Josh Rubin shout. "Hit it outta here!"

Brian wished his mom had been around for some of the great feelings that came with the streak, especially if it was about to end. But his mom didn't care much about baseball, and she never came to the games. Today she'd gone off to an art gallery with his older sister, Barbara. Barbara was good at painting, and his mom liked art and all that kind of stuff much better than she liked sports.

His parents had split up when he was two, so his dad wasn't around either.

Jeff Rothenberg, the Wildcat pitcher, was winding up. Brian watched him, watched the ball come over the top, concentrated extra hard so he could block out the thoughts he didn't like.

The ball thwacked into the catcher's mitt. High and outside. Ball 1.

Brian stepped out and tapped the dirt off his sneakers with the end of his bat. Rothenberg was the second relief pitcher of the day for the Wildcats. He had a good fastball and good control. He'd come in in the top of the fourth when the Rockets had exploded for four of their eight runs. He'd quieted things down, and he had kept them quiet. Now, with two out, he'd given up those back-to-back singles.

Brian stepped in. Rothenberg seemed a little fidgety. He walked around on the mound, adjusting and readjusting his cap. Holding the runners, pitching from the set position, he hurled another fastball.

Brian watched it all the way. He thought it was low and off the inside corner, but the umpire called, "Strike one!"

That seemed to give Rothenberg confidence. He threw a change-up that Brian fouled back, then a fastball that missed by a mile.

2 and 2. Things were tightening up.

"Stay in there!" Justin yelled from the bench.

"Protect the plate!" yelled Andy McClellan.

Brian looked down to Jack Carr, coaching at third base. Mr. Carr was wiping his shirt, then clapping. Good. Clapping meant hit away. There wasn't anything else he could do in this situation. A squeeze play was too risky.

Brian settled in, got ready. Luke was dancing down the line at third, making Rothenberg crazy. A throw over. A throw over again. Then the pitch.

It was a fastball, a little outside at the letters, and Brian knew it was his. He strode into it, snapped his wrists, felt the ball fly off his bat heading for left field. He took off for first, hoping it would drop.

It did. The left fielder, running hard, had to scoop it up on the short hop. As Brian reached first base and made the turn, he saw Luke score standing up. He kept on going and so did Phil, barreling in to third on the

6

late throw to the plate. But Phil overran the bag! The Wildcat catcher fired down. Phil was out, trying to dive back to third.

Well, so what? thought Brian, trotting in to pick up his glove. It was true you should never make the third out at third base. It was more true you should never make it in such a dumb way, but at least they'd scored the extra run, hadn't they? He'd kept his streak alive, hadn't he?

Wooo, that felt good!

As he reached the dugout, Phil was there, looking terrible. His eyes focused on the ground.

"Sorry I screwed up, Brian."

"Forget it, Phil. We got the run. Let's win the game."

Phil smiled a little. His eyes brightened.

"Good going with the streak!" someone said.

Brian turned, and it was Luke. "Thanks, man."

They exchanged a big high-five.

"Going for DiMaggio's record?"

"Yeah, sure."

A few pokes in the ribs, and all three trotted back onto the field.

2. Fits and Errors

Justin didn't do so well starting out the bottom of the sixth. He walked the first batter on four pitches, and after a pop-up, Linda Hurley, the Wildcat center fielder, singled that first batter over to third. Tommy Berditch, the catcher, struck out, but no one could breathe easy. Coming to the plate was a big black kid named George Coleman. He was the Wildcats' cleanup man, their toughest power hitter.

George had gone two for three with a home run so far today. He crowded the plate, swept his arms back, and glared.

Justin wasn't flustered for a moment. Working in his slow way, he brought the count to 1 and 1. But this time his slow delivery went against him. He looked the runners back at first and third, threw over once or twice, but even pitching from the stretch, he took a little too long. On Ball 2, Linda Hurley stole second base.

Now there were runners on second and third with two out. George Coleman, the tying run, was still at the plate.

The Rockets were nervous, but this was the moment to settle down. One more out was all they needed. One more out was what they had to get.

Brian tried to talk it up in the infield. "Come on, Justin, do it!" he shouted, pounding his glove.

"Yeah, do it!" said Josh Rubin at first.

"Yeah, do it!" said Vicky Lopez at second.

Justin stood quietly on the mound, and Brian got himself ready. He bent his knees with his feet wide apart, leaned forward on the balls of his feet, dangled his arms in front of him with his glove open toward the batter. "Hit the ball to me, George," he said to himself. "Hit the ball to me!"

But he was also thinking about keeping his streak alive. Eleven straight games! And the Rockets would win this game. What a great feeling!

George Coleman connected. A sharply hit ground ball was coming right at Brian! He charged it, got his fanny down and the fingers of his glove on the ground in front of him. This was going to be an easy out, but the ball took a bad hop and bounced off his chest. He knocked it down, he still had the play, but he'd been so distracted, he panicked. Brian Krause, the best fielder on the Raymondtown Rockets, threw wildly to first, and two runs scored.

The Wildcat fans went crazy. It was now 9–8, with a runner in scoring position at second base.

Brian tried not to look around the infield. He could hardly believe he had done what he'd done, but there was nothing he could say about it now. They still had to get the next batter out. They still had to win the game.

He slapped his fist into his glove. "Come on, Justin, do it!" he said again. Then he added, "We'll get 'em this time."

Justin didn't look at him. He wound and threw a meatball down the middle of the plate!

Corky Lewis, the Wildcat third baseman, swung. The ball exploded off his bat. It was high and deep to right. It was going, going—

Brian watched in horror. George Coleman was already trotting home. Corky Lewis was reaching second base. If the ball landed in the bleachers, Brian's error would have cost the Rockets the game.

But Pete Wyshansky was drifting over, drifting over, getting under it. He reached up and caught the ball before it could clear the right field fence.

The game was over. The Rockets had won 9–8.

"Rah rah Rockets!" the small group of Raymondtown fans yelled.

The winning team ran off the field, high-fiving each other right and left. Only Brian Krause stood where he was, in his shortstop's position. Someone running in patted him on the fanny, but even then, he didn't move. He'd never felt such relief, but he was also trying to sort out his thoughts.

Finally he trudged into the dugout and joined his teammates for the ritual shaking of hands with the Wildcats at home plate. No one was very enthusiastic. The Wildcats seemed more bewildered than defeated, and when the whole thing was over, Brian slumped onto the visitors' bench.

The rest of the Rockets were getting their gear together, but Luke came over and sat beside him. He bumped him on the shoulder.

"What's up, DiMadge?"

Brian shrugged.

"Look," Luke said, "I know how you're feeling. Nobody likes to make errors, but it was just a bad break. You never make errors like that. Not you. Not surehands Krause. And we won the game, remember? We almost blew it, but we won!"

Brian looked at Luke. He hated being reminded of his error. Couldn't Luke remind him of his streak instead? Without even thinking, he said, "Who cares about the error? My streak's the best thing that ever happened to this team!"

Luke looked stunned. His mouth dropped open, and he stood up. "Well, excuse me, DiMadge," he said. Then he walked away.

Brian knew he'd said the wrong thing the moment the words were out of his mouth. He wanted to take them back, but it was too late. But weren't the words sort of true, too? His error had almost cost them the game, but wasn't it his hit that had driven in what turned out to be the winning run? That was the hit that continued the streak, so wasn't it important?

Brian realized he was trying to make excuses for what he'd said, but he couldn't help it. He was really embarrassed about the whole scene and knew he'd offended Luke. Would Luke talk to Phil about what he'd said? Would they both think he was a show-off who didn't care about the team?

Coach Channing walked by and smiled. "Good work continuing the streak, Brian."

"Thanks, coach."

There. That was how it should be. Everyone should be proud of his streak and forget about his error!

3. Nobody Home

A car horn blared from the parking lot. It was Luke's father in the ancient blue Buick. Depending on who was available, Mr. Emory or Mr. Hubbard drove Luke, Phil, and Brian to their away games. Brian wasn't going to escape Luke and Phil so easily. He would have to take the long drive home with them.

He got his gear organized and headed for the parking lot. Only a few cars were left, and he noticed the battered Buick over to one side. He approached slowly. Mr. Emory was behind the wheel. Luke and Phil were already in the back.

Brian swung open the front door and squeezed onto the high seat. Mr. Emory hardly looked at him, just started the engine and pulled out into traffic.

At first Brian thought Luke's father was mad at him, too. Then he realized this was just Mr. Emory's gruffly casual way. The boys in the back seemed wrapped in gloom, but a moment later Mr. Emory began a conversation.

"High-scoring game today, Brian."

"Yeah. It was a tough one."

"But you kids held on. Bit of a scare in the sixth inning, though."

"Yeah. I was pretty worried when that ball looked like it was going out."

"Kept your hitting streak alive, didn't you?"

"Yes, sir. I was upset about my error, though."

Mr. Emory was friendly, warm, easy to talk to. He also knew his baseball. Brian didn't even mind mentioning his error to him, but just after he did, there was a little pause.

Phil leaned over. "The error wasn't so bad, Brian. I did worse when I overran the bag!"

Brian knew Luke had been talking to Phil, and that Phil was trying to lead the

17

way toward patching things up. But there had been that awkward silence in the backseat, and Phil was dwelling on the error all over again. Comparing it with his own dumb mistake somehow made it worse.

Tight-lipped, not even believing what he was saying, Brian hissed, "I don't care about the error. All I care about is my streak!"

Phil fell back. Luke disappeared into the corner by the window. Mr. Emory glanced over at Brian, then returned his gaze to the windshield and the traffic.

There was no more conversation. Mr. Emory drove and drove. The boys all looked out the windows. Brian couldn't believe he'd done it again, this time with Phil *and* Luke. He knew it was because he was still in a crummy mood about the error, but now he'd gone and made everything worse.

When the car pulled into Market Street and stopped in front of his building, Brian jumped out, said "Thanks, Mr. Emory," and slammed the door. No one else said anything.

The car pulled away from the curb. Brian watched it go, wondering if most of his good times were going with it. When he could no longer see the taillights in the distance, he unlocked his front door and trudged up the dark stairs to his apartment.

The apartment was on the second floor, just above Bickerton's Drug Store. It had three small bedrooms, a living room, and a kitchen with a big round table. Brian was glad he had his own room, but since most of his friends lived in houses, he felt weird to be living downtown in an apartment.

Even so, it was home, but as he reached the top of the stairs and went inside, his heart sank. The silence of the rooms echoed the silence of the car. No one was home but him.

Usually Brian didn't mind being home by himself. Today he minded. He needed to talk about the streak and the error and how he'd messed things up afterwards. Even if his mom and Barbara couldn't get to the game, couldn't they have gotten home before him?

Brian went into the kitchen and sat down at the big round table. Then he got up, poured himself a Coke, and sat down again.

He sat, sipping and thinking, until there was a commotion in the hall.

He got up, and the front door burst open. "Brian, we're home!" his mother shouted. She raced into the kitchen, dumping bags of groceries on the table.

"Brian, what are you doing in this dark kitchen? I'm sorry we're home so late. There was this humongous line at the supermarket!"

She hugged him. Everything felt a whole lot better. Barbara was there, too, and she hugged him. It wasn't as terrific as Mom's, but it wasn't so bad either.

Now, maybe, they could talk about this afternoon.

"Brian," said his mom, "why don't you and Barbara get started on your homework. I'll fix dinner. I'll call you both when it's ready."

"But, Mom—" Brian said.

"Not another word. I want that homework done. We're having chicken and carrots, something you both like. Oh, by the way, how was the game?"

"We won," Brian said.

"Terrific! Congratulations! You can tell us all about it at dinner. Now march!"

Brian took a shower. Then he sat at his desk and puzzled over math problems and vocabulary words and what would happen to his role on the team now that Luke and Phil were mad at him. He puzzled over his mom, who was pretty and had red hair like his and was so often out to lunch. And then there was Barbara, who was okay but awkward and difficult. Perhaps that's what it was like when you were a twelve-year-old girl.

"Brian! Barbara!"

Brian hurried to the table. He really did like chicken and carrots, and it was especially good tonight.

"We had a great time at the gallery," Mom said between bites. "It was an exhibition of French Impressionists—they were artists who painted their own impressions of the real world—and it was fabulous. There was a wonderful Monet and two Renoirs and a van Gogh."

"I liked it, too," Barbara said.

"So much light, so much color," said Mom.

"I bet Barbara's painting will be as good as that someday."

Barbara blushed. "Oh, Mom—"

"It's true. You've got real talent. But, Brian, you would have liked this exhibition, too. I wish you would come with us sometime."

"I can't come when it's baseball season," Brian said.

"I know. This baseball business just swallows you up."

"I kept my hitting streak alive today, Mom. Eleven straight games."

"Well, that's good."

"But, Mom, there was something—"

"Wait! Let me get dessert."

She was gone, then back in a moment with a fresh blueberry pie.

"Mom," Brian began again.

"Wait just another moment," Mom said. "Wait until I finish serving, please."

With great energy, she scooped out the portions of blueberry pie and passed them around. Then she looked over at Brian and squinted.

"Brian," she said, "I know you had a

23

shower, but you seem to have missed a large smudge on your cheek. Could you please wash it off before we have dessert?"

Furious, Brian rushed to the bathroom. He looked in the mirror. There it was, yet another offending piece of dirt. He scrubbed it off, rushed back to the table, dug into his blueberry pie.

"Now what was it you wanted to tell me?" Mom asked.

Brian looked up, his mouth full. "Nothing," he said. "It wasn't important."

4. A Change in Plan

Brian was in the *other* third grade class. It wasn't really called that. It was just Brian who thought of it that way.

Mrs. Carey was his teacher and he liked her a lot, but except for Michael Wong and Vicky Lopez and the substitutes Adam Spinelli and Jordan Smithers, the rest of the Rockets were in Mrs. Irvington's class across the hall. Brian knew this hadn't been done on purpose. After all, classes had been underway since the fall and tryouts for the Rockets hadn't even been held until the beginning of April. Even so, he felt isolated from his teammates, as if, somehow, a weird stroke of fate had made him less favored and less important than they.

Walking into school this Monday morning, he felt worse than usual. It no longer mattered that he was set apart. His best friends on the team thought he was a jerk.

Luckily his seat was near the back of the room. He felt too bad to want to say anything in class, and he hoped against hope that Mrs. Carey wouldn't call on him.

She didn't. Suddenly everyone was getting ready for gym.

The trouble was the two third grades had gym together. Would he be able to avoid Luke and Phil?

Wait a minute. Didn't he really want to see them and make it all up? He had no idea what he could say. Would anything make a difference?

They were way up front in gym class. He was way in the back. There was no chance even to say hello.

But lunch was coming up. Brian sat in a corner of the cafetorium, hoping no one would notice he was there. He ate his tuna sandwich and a little dish of canned peaches. As he was finishing the peaches, he glanced up.

"Hey," said Luke, "isn't that the boy with the eleven-game hitting streak?"

"Why, yes," said Phil, "I do believe it is. If he could only hold onto the baseball, we'd be sure to win every game."

Tears welled up in the corners of Brian's eyes. He jumped up and ran back to Mrs. Carey's room.

He couldn't wait for school to end. As soon as the bell rang, he was out of his chair, putting on his jacket. He usually walked home anyway, and this time he walked quickly, hoping no one he knew would catch up with him and want to talk.

It was a beautiful spring afternoon, not too warm and very sunny. He could smell the sweetness of the trees and the grass. It was a perfect day for baseball.

But Brian was glad to have a day away from baseball. He was also glad to have a day away from his friends, if he could still call them that. He needed to relax, hang out, clear his head.

By the time he reached Market Street, he was no longer hurrying. He was strolling, having a good time looking in shop windows and watching people. But when he reached his block, he began hurrying again. His mother got off work at four o'clock. She'd probably be home by now!

He raced up the stairs and flung open the apartment door. The emptiness, the quiet, engulfed him once again. He ran into the kitchen. A note was on the big round table.

Brian recognized his mother's handwriting.

"Dear Brian and Barbara," he read, "I'm sorry I won't be home for dinner. I'm going out with a new friend. There's food in the fridge. I won't be late. Love you both, Mom."

Brian sat down hard. A "new friend" could mean only one thing: a new boyfriend. Brian didn't exactly object to these new boyfriends when they appeared. It was just that when they disappeared, which they always did, his mom ended up miserable. They also meant he had less time than ever to spend with his mom, and sometimes the boyfriends didn't even like him!

And now there would be another one.

Though he'd enjoyed walking home by himself, he now felt terribly alone. He had an eleven-game hitting streak going, the best in the Tri-City Junior League. He wanted to be proud of that, wanted his friends to be proud of it with him. He remembered when he and Luke helped Phil practice enough so he could make the Rockets. He remembered when he and Phil and Vicky Lopez helped Luke break out of his slump. It was great to know they needed each other. What could he do to win them back?

Brian heard the front door open softly. Was his mother coming home for dinner after all? No, she never opened a door softly. It had to be his sister.

Barbara walked into the kitchen. "What's going on?"

Brian handed her the note.

"Oh," she said, reading it with her head cocked to one side. She smiled. "I guess this means we get to fend for ourselves."

The smile was the nicest thing that had happened to Brian all day. Was his sister usually like this? He couldn't remember.

He smiled back. "I guess so."

"Well, we better get started. Will you help?"

"Of course."

Together they opened the fridge. They found cold cuts in waxed paper and some salad in a bowl with a jar of homemade dressing beside it. There was a bottle of soda and a long loaf of bread.

Barbara arranged the cold cuts on a plate. Brian cut up some of the bread and mixed the dressing into the salad. Then he poured them each a glass of soda while Barbara lit a candle for the table.

"What's that for?" Brian asked.

"Atmosphere," said Barbara.

He had to admit she had a point. When they sat down side by side, it all felt pretty cozy. It was also great to have done something together. Teamwork, like on the Rockets. The food tasted pretty good, too.

Afterwards, Brian and Barbara did the dishes. She washed. He dried.

"Please be careful putting away those plates," she said as he reached high for a cabinet.

"I know, I know," he said, not even minding being bossed around a little.

When they were through, Barbara said, "Want to see something I did today?"

"Sure, why not?" Brian said.

They went into Barbara's room. On the easel by the window was a big watercolor painting. It was a field full of red trees and purple clouds, with a golden yellow sun and a lot of light. All the brush strokes were tiny dots of paint.

"It's great," said Brian.

"It's pointillism," said Barbara. "That's why there are dots. It's one of the techniques the Impressionists used."

"I like it."

"Would you like to have it? You could hang it in your room."

Brian was overwhelmed. "Sure. Thanks, Barbara."

There wasn't much space on Brian's wall. He had to take down the poster of the 1927 New York Yankees and the photograph of Ozzie Smith, the great shortstop for the St. Louis Cardinals. But when they'd put up the painting—carefully, with little rolls of tape behind each corner of the paper—it looked terrific.

"See?" said Barbara. "You're starting to

31

like art. Will you come to the museum next time?"

"If there's no practice," Brian said. Then he added, "Barbara, do you think you could like baseball? I mean, just a little. It's as exciting as painting."

Barbara shrugged.

"I'd love it if you came and watched me play. There are girls on our team and everything."

Barbara looked away. "Baseball always seems so boring, but"—there was that smile again—"anything's possible."

5. Practice Makes Perfect

Tuesday morning. School again. For the first time Mrs. Carey's class seemed like an advantage. He wouldn't have to look at Luke and Phil all day long. All he had to do was steer clear of them at gym and lunch and again at music. That couldn't be so hard to do.

It wasn't. He ignored them in gym, stayed on the other side of the cafetorium at lunch, and sat with Jordan Smithers at music. Luke and Phil seemed to realize they should stay away. They didn't take a step in his direction.

Finally the bell rang. As Brian sat at his locker, changing his clothes for practice, Pete Wyshansky appeared.

"Hey, Brian?"

"Yes, Pete."

"Maybe you could have another kind of

streak. Say, a big hit every game and a big error to go with it."

Brian smirked. "Thanks for your confidence, Pete."

His stomach rolled. Already Pete was walking off, satisfied with his effect. But Pete was nasty to everyone. How could Brian take him seriously? This was the moment to fight back and try harder. He pulled on his shirt and headed for the ballfield.

He worked very hard that day. Coach Lopez was hitting ground balls to the infielders, and he worked especially hard on them. He made sure he charged in, got down, got in front of the ball, got his glove down, looked the ball into the glove, timed the release of his throw to first. He worked on the double play with Vicky Lopez, taking the feed and firing to first when the ball came to the right side, giving the feed to Vicky when the ball came to the left. He practiced moving to his right with the crossover step, backhanding the ball, and making the long throw to first. He practiced diving to his left, cutting off that base hit up the middle. Then he caught some pop-ups and went and threw some pitches off the practice rubber. He was seldom asked to start a game, but he never knew when he might be needed in relief.

Through it all, he kept his mouth shut, even when he was playing short and Phil was playing third. It seemed the best way, the only way, for the moment.

Afterwards, Coach Channing called everyone into the dugout. "I'm sorry," he said, "but there's been another schedule change. Again the Bombers can't play on Sunday, so that game will be played in Healesville tomorrow at three-thirty. I hope that won't cause transportation problems for any of you. Let me know if you're stuck."

Oh, no, Brian thought. If he wasn't even speaking to Luke and Phil, how could he make plans to go to the game with them?

It seemed that Coach Channing was making these announcements almost every week now. They were always playing Wednesday games, with fewer fans and less time for practice and homework. Even so, he'd have a chance to continue his streak!

If only there were some other way of getting to Healesville.

He'd think about it tomorrow. Now he

was going home. He'd been sitting around so long, the rest of the team had left. Picking up his bat and glove, straightening his cap, he was surprised to hear voices as he crossed the parking lot.

Coach Channing was standing beside his old green Ford. A bald little man with a pot belly, Adam Spinelli's father, was gesturing in front of him.

The coach had his car keys in his hand and the door open. Clearly Mr. Spinelli was keeping him from leaving.

Brian moved a little closer and saw Adam. He was standing a few feet away, looking embarrassed.

"Mr. Spinelli," the coach was saying, "I'd love to start your son tomorrow, but there are nine other kids ahead of him. He's playing well, playing better, but he missed a few practices back there and the starting team's pretty well set now—"

"Mr. Channing," said Mr. Spinelli, "my boy is a good player. He has practiced hard. He deserves a chance. Even if he doesn't start, he should play more. You're keeping him from playing!"

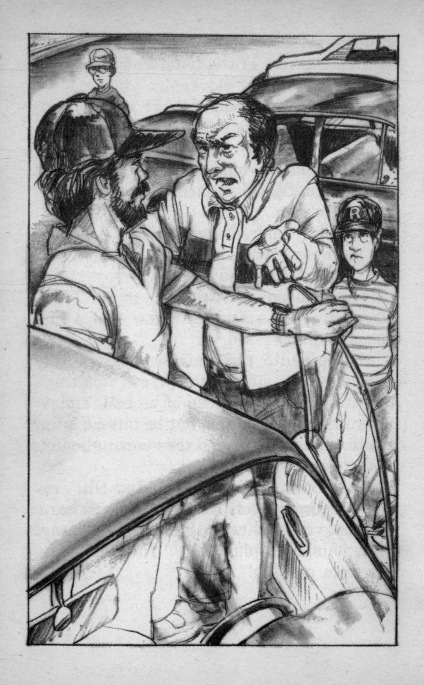

"I'm sorry. That simply isn't true. Now if you'll excuse me, I'm very tired and I want to go home."

Coach Channing stepped into his car, closed the door, and started the engine. Then he backed out of his space, turned, and drove off.

Mr. Spinelli and Adam were left where they were standing. Adam walked over to his father and put his arm around him "Thanks, Dad, but the coach makes his own decisions. You can't force him into anything."

"Who's forcing? You're a good player. He should know that."

"I hope he will. Maybe by the end of the season."

They walked over to a white Honda and drove off.

Brian waited until the car had disappeared. Then he hurried out of the parking lot and walked the five blocks down Market Street to home.

Adam Spinelli had started only one game—against the Hurricanes a while ago. After this scene, would Coach Channing *ever* let him start again?

6. A Beginning

Full of news, Brian bounded up the stairs. As he flung open the door, his mom shouted from the kitchen, "Surprise!"

Brian froze. Then he tossed his bat and glove into his room and walked very slowly, practically on tiptoe, to the kitchen.

At the stove was a large, beefy-looking guy with brown hair. He was wearing a long white apron and stirring some vegetables with a wooden spoon.

Mom fussed around him, adding spices to a large fish she was cooking in a pan. "Brian," she said, "there's someone I want you to meet."

The large, beefy-looking man held out his hand. He had a big smile and small blue eyes. "Hi," he said. "Mickey Jennings. Pleased to meet you."

Brian introduced himself and shook hands. The handshake hurt.

"Mickey's one of the new insurance agents at work," Mom said, "and I've invited him for dinner. I hope you boys will like each other."

Oh, brother, thought Brian. Barbara was sitting in the corner. She rolled her eyes.

Mom bustled about, setting the table, checking the fish on the stove, making sure everything was just right. Barbara and Brian helped her. Finally they all sat down to eat.

"I hope this is good," said Mom, patting her hair.

"Oh, I'm sure it will be," said Mickey Jennings. "It looks delicious."

Brian decided not to comment, but there wasn't much chance anyway. Mom and Mickey Jennings talked about work and insurance and the not-so-terrific place Mickey Jennings was staying until he got himself located. All Brian and Barbara got to do was look at each other across the table and wonder what it would be like if Mickey Jennings became part of their future.

41

At least the food was good. Mom was a wonderful cook, and after they had finished the main course, she served a special fruit salad she had made for dessert.

As everyone dug in, Mickey Jennings said, "So what do you like to do, Brian?"

It seemed like a dumb question. "I like school," Brian said. "I play baseball."

"What position?" said Mickey Jennings.

"I'm the starting shortstop on the Raymondtown Rockets. I bat fifth, and I've got an eleven-game hitting streak, the longest in the league."

"That's pretty impressive. I used to play some ball myself. Third base, mostly. Got scouted by the pros in college, but I hurt my knee. That ended that."

"You almost made it to the show? That's neat."

"Well, I wouldn't say that exactly. They'd have sent me to the minors first. It's a long way to the show from the minors."

"You must have been good."

"I wasn't bad."

For an hour they talked baseball, as if they were old friends. They talked infield

plays and batting averages and what gloves they liked best. They talked teams and teammates and players in the majors and who had won the pennants in 1981 and 1985 and who had won the Series those same years. By the time Brian excused him-self to do his homework, he had sort of a different idea about this guy Mickey.

7. An Ending

But how was he going to get to the game in Healesville? Everyone knew he always went with Luke and Phil. He was embarrassed to ask anyone else.

At lunchtime the next day, Brian summoned up his courage. Luke and Phil were at a table in the middle of the cafetorium. He walked over and said, "Hi, do I still have a lift for today?"

Phil looked up. "My mom's driving. Meet us after school."

"Maybe you can get another base hit in the car," Luke said.

"Thanks," Brian said. "I won't keep you waiting."

He walked away. The conversation had been less than terrific, but at least he had a ride.

He was the first one out to the car after school. He recognized the Volvo and Mrs. Hubbard's blond hair and jumped into the front seat with his stuff. He had only had time to say hello when Luke and Phil piled into the back.

Silence again, the same silence as last time. Mrs. Hubbard switched on the radio. When they were almost in Healesville, she said, "Is something the matter with you boys? Have you lost your tongues?"

"Preparing for the game," Luke said.

"Listening for the ball meeting Brian's bat," said Phil.

"I see," said Mrs. Hubbard.

It was time to play ball. The boys tumbled out of the car and onto the Bombers' field. The infield grass was too high, and there were pebbles in the base paths. Coach Channing complained to the Bomber coach that the pitcher's mound was much too low to be regulation height. There was practically no mound at all, he said.

"Take it or leave it," said the Bomber coach.

The Rockets took it. It was hard enough

to schedule a game with this team, and they'd driven all the way to Healesville. They did their stretches and warm-up wind sprints and ran out for fielding practice.

Coach Lopez was hitting ground balls to the infield. Brian noticed how the ball seemed to die in the high grass, but he figured out how to charge it, collar it, and get off a good throw to first before it stopped in front of him. He felt he had his rhythm back, that he'd have a good day. So what if he didn't talk to Luke and Phil? They'd still make the plays. He felt good at the plate, too, when he took his licks. He was ready to pound the ball and keep his streak alive.

When he checked the lineup card, he noticed that Adam Spinelli wasn't starting.

That seemed sad, but it was hardly a surprise. Hardly a surprise either was the presence of Fred Pelsky on the mound for the Bombers.

Pelsky was the same junk pitcher they had faced when they played the Bombers at home. Chubby, with a pink face and straggly hair, he specialized in high looping change-ups that somehow always seemed to catch the corner of the plate. Then, just to make sure he'd upset your timing, he'd mix in a fastball or two. The Rockets had gotten to him in the bottom of the fifth in the last game, but it was only by some miracle that they had.

From the beginning, it didn't look like any miracles were happening today. Luke came up and popped out to third base. Phil fanned, and Andy McClellan, playing left field for Jenny Carr, bounced a weak grounder to second.

Then it was the Bombers' turn. Little Josh Rubin was starting for the Rockets. He was really pumped, stalking around on what there was of a mound and hollering after every pitch. His sidearm heater was finding the corners, too. He struck out the first batter, and the second skyed to right.

Vicky Lopez was egging him on. "Go, Josh, go! Let's go, Rockets!"

But as Jim Bostwick, the Bombers' heavy-hitting third baseman, stepped in, Brian sensed trouble. Bostwick fouled off the first two pitches; then Josh got sloppy. The count ran to 3 and 2.

"Come on, Josh!" Brian shouted. "One more strike!"

"Yeah, one more!" shouted Justin Carr from first.

"Yeah, just one!" Phil Hubbard yelled from third.

Josh wound and threw. It was a sidearm fastball, low on the outside corner, and it surprised Bostwick completely. A left-handed batter, he lunged—and just got a piece of it.

A squibbed ground ball scooted down the third base line. Phil charged it, expecting an easy play, but trapped by the high grass, the ball stopped before it reached him. He dug it out and made the throw, but his timing was completely off. The ball soared past Justin's outstretched mitt, and Bostwick ended up at second.

Josh was not happy about this at all. He stalked around even more than before, touched his cap, fixed his shirt. Brian came out to settle him down, but whatever he said didn't do much good.

And slugging Steve Paretti was coming to the plate.

Josh checked the runner at second. Nervously, pitching from the stretch, he fired Ball 1. Then he fired Ball 2.

Brian went over to talk. "Relax, Josh. Easy does it. Just throw strikes."

"Right," said Josh. "Okay. No problem."

Brian went back to short, took a deep breath, got ready. He needn't have bothered. The next pitch was a fastball down and away, exactly what Paretti wanted. He crushed it over the center field fence.

Josh's shoulders slumped as the runners cleared the bases. Luke came out. Brian and Vicky went over. Luke and Brian didn't look at each other, but that was okay.

Josh was such a trooper. He put his glove on his hip and smiled. "Hey, guys, here for a party? Why don't we wait till I've struck out this next sucker?"

And that was what he did. He hurled three fastballs past center fielder Larry Cain, and the Bombers were through.

But they were ahead 2–0, and the Rockets still had to face Pelsky. Justin led off the top of the second and grounded to short. Then it was Brian's turn.

First at bat. Watched Pelsky closely. Ran the count to 2 and 1. Fouled one back. Popped up to third.

Definitely not wonderful. It seemed even less wonderful when Pete Wyshansky struck out swinging.

In the bottom of the second the Bombers capitalized once more on the mess that was their field. Josh got the first two outs on ground balls. Then Johnny O'Brien, the little second baseman, lifted one to left.

Andy went back. He wasn't used to playing left field, and he'd certainly never played it in the midst of roots and weeds and stones. He got his feet tangled up. He dropped the ball.

Johnny O'Brien was fast. He got all the way to second before Andy recovered. Then, of course, the next batter singled to right, and the run scored.

But that was all the Bombers would get that inning, and it was all they would get that day. Josh settled down after that and pitched well into the fifth. Then Brian relieved him, gave up a one-out single to

52

Steve Paretti, and set down the next two batters with a minimum of fuss.

The only trouble was the Rocket bats had gone completely cold. Pelsky was so sharp, they got only two more hits until the top of the sixth.

Brian couldn't believe it, and he was even less happy about himself. Second at bat. Fourth inning. Arms back. Crouch. Watch the ball. Popped up to the catcher.

He was hitting under the ball, and he couldn't figure out why.

The top of the sixth brought a flurry of hope. Vicky Lopez bounced a single over Johnny O'Brien's head, and Luke walked. Then Phil singled to drive in Vicky, Luke and Phil advanced on a passed ball, and Justin struck out. Brian came to the plate with runners on second and third and one down.

It was his last chance to keep his streak alive. A homer would mean the winning run. A double would tie it at 3.

Brian stepped in. He swung on the first pitch and fouled it back.

"Relax!" Coach Channing shouted. "You're way out in front!"

Brian thought he was relaxed. He got into his stance, faced Pelsky, let a pitch go by, ran the count to 2 and 1. Then he popped up to the first baseman.

He was horrified, so horrified he could hardly return to the bench. But he did, trying to keep out of everyone's way, and he sat and watched as Pete Wyshansky flied out to end the game. Then, over in the corner by himself, he took off his glasses, put his head in his hands, and began to cry.

8. Pizza and Pointers

He had felt so good about his streak, felt he could just go on hitting despite the troubles with Luke and Phil. Now it was over, and he hurt so bad.

Coach Channing put his arm around him. "Brian," he said, "come on. You had a bad day at the plate, that's all. You'll have another streak. Besides, you had an excellent day in the field."

Brian dried his eyes. It was true. Despite that terrible infield, he'd made several good plays at short. He'd also pitched pretty well.

"All right, everyone," Coach Channing said. "Pack up your gear and find your rides. We're having pizza at Angelo's as soon as you can get there!"

From hope to despair. With his streak down the tubes, how could Brian ride over to Angelo's with Luke and Phil? Even though Phil had made that error today, they'd never leave him alone.

"Want a lift?"

It was Adam Spinelli, looking sheepish.

"Sure," said Brian. "Don't you have a full car?"

"No. We've got room."

"I'd better let Mrs. Hubbard know."

She was standing with Luke and Phil. When Brian explained he was going to ride with Adam, Luke said, "Sorry about the streak, Brian."

"Yeah, sorry," Phil said.

Brian nodded. "Thanks, guys." Then he went off with Adam.

There was no one else riding with the Spinellis, and it quickly became clear why. The entire ride to Angelo's, Adam buried himself in the backseat and Mr. Spinelli carried on about how the coach was ignoring his son.

"He should be starting! At least he should be playing. He didn't play at all today!"

By the time they got out of the car, Brian's head was spinning. He was grateful when Mr. Spinelli said he would be going home, not having pizza, but he wasn't prepared for what happened when he and Adam got inside the door.

"I'm sorry, Brian," Adam said. "My father gets carried away sometimes. I know I'm not good enough to start."

"Hey, it's okay," Brian said, smiling. "Let's go eat pizza."

They sat down together. As the hot pies were passed around, Coach Channing said, "You all deserve this. You played really well under terrible conditions, and you were good sports throughout. Three to one is not a bad score under the circumstances, and I know you're going to have a great game Saturday. Just remember, one slice each. I don't want your mothers calling, saying you couldn't eat dinner."

"You know," Adam said between mouthfuls, "I think we've got a pretty good team."

"Yeah, I think so, too," Brian replied.

"I think you're one of the best, though."

"You do?"

"Yeah. You hit for average. You're good

in the clutch. You pitch well in relief. You don't make a lot of errors."

"Thanks."

"I'm sorry about the streak."

It almost didn't matter anymore. "That's okay," Brian said. "I just wish we'd won the game."

"We'll win Saturday."

"Yeah."

They kept talking until they had to leave. It was mostly about the team and baseball, but after a while they even talked about Mrs. Carey and what a good teacher they thought she was.

Brian raced home, took the stairs two at a time. Mickey was there again, wearing the same apron.

"He was in the neighborhood," Mom said. "How could I turn him away?"

Mickey and Brian slapped hands. "How did it go today, sport?"

"We lost," Brian said. "The field was terrible. I couldn't get a hit nohow."

"Tough luck. Want to talk about it?"

"Yeah."

They sat on the living room sofa. "You

must be disappointed about the streak," Mickey said.

"I was," said Brian, "but I'm not anymore. Well, maybe a little."

He described how awful he'd felt after the game, how Coach Channing had cheered him up and becoming friends with Adam Spinelli had made the difference.

"Good going," Mickey said. "You're learning how to take your lumps and bounce back. Let's go tell your mom about this new friend."

Mom was very interested in Adam Spinelli. "Who is he?" she asked. "Do I know the family?"

Brian explained. Mom didn't know the Spinellis. Neither did Barbara, but the atmosphere around the dinner table couldn't have been more upbeat.

60

9. Dinner Isn't the Point

Thursday at school whizzed by. With Mrs. Carey's permission, Adam moved his desk to an empty one near Brian's. Over lunch, the two of them talked some more. Adam, it turned out, loved fishing. Would Brian like to join him and his dad sometime this summer?

Brian wasn't so sure about Mr. Spinelli, but the idea sounded great. "Sure," he said, "I'd love to."

"Then we'll do it."

As school let out, Brian was getting ready to go home when Adam said, "Why don't you come by my house?"

"Hey, terrific!" said Brian, "and why don't we get some practicing in, too?"

"Neat," said Adam. "I've got a big backyard."

There were trees at the far end and lots of room in between. At first they just played catch, gradually drifting farther and farther apart. Then Brian got into gear.

"Do you want me to give you some pointers?"

"I was hoping you might," said Adam.

Brian began by throwing grounders. Then, as Adam grew more confident, he began fungoing them. He explained how Adam needed to bend his knees more, that he really needed to get down, get his glove under the ball, not bend so much from the waist.

Working on the grounders, they also worked on Adam's throwing. Brian showed him how to be sure to point his throwing shoulder toward the target, keep the rhythm, shift his weight and snap the ball as he threw. Over and over they practiced, and then they switched to hitting.

They made a makeshift home plate, batter's box, and pitcher's mound. Brian got Adam into his stance, showed him how to anchor his back foot, bring back his arms, keep his head down, shift his weight, stride

forward, concentrate. All these things had been part of team practices, but Adam hadn't been given such personal attention before. When he was ready, Brian pitched to him. The results got better and better.

Afterwards, Adam was a little winded. "Thanks, Brian. That was the best."

"I'm glad. I had fun, too," Brian said. "Practicing with you helped me get my confidence back."

"You shouldn't need much more of that."

"I did after yesterday."

Mrs. Spinelli drove Brian home. As they pulled into Market Street, he thought of Luke and Phil. He had to do something about that. He just wasn't sure what or when.

Friday. School and then practice. Brian had his usual good workout, worked extra hard on his hitting. The familiar line drives were falling in again. His timing was back. Whatever was wrong on Wednesday seemed to have gone away.

He couldn't help noticing that Adam Spinelli was doing better, too.

Home for dinner. No one but Mom and

Barbara. As they were finishing dessert, Mom said, "Oh, by the way, Brian, there's a one-day exhibition at the museum tomorrow. Barbara and I are going. Mickey said he might come, too."

"Oh, Mom," Brian said, "tomorrow's our game against the Rams. Just this once, I wanted you to come!"

"I'm sorry, Brian. We'll just have to have a great dinner afterwards. The three of us will be home before you are."

"Dinner isn't the point."

"We'll have burgers and fries. Your favorites."

"Okay, okay."

That night Brian tossed around in bed, looking at his sister's painting. Would she ever get interested in baseball? Would his mom? It seemed pretty hopeless.

10. A Little Bit Extra

The next day Brian arrived at the ball-park early. Luke was there already, and they exchanged gruff hellos. Moments later, it seemed, everyone else appeared. The Rockets did their warm-ups and trotted onto the field.

When fielding and hitting practice was over, Brian relaxed on the bench in the home team dugout. It was a cool and sunny Saturday, a great day for baseball. He watched the stands filling up with Rockets fans, frowned when he saw a green and gold Rams cap.

Mr. Spinelli appeared. He found a front row seat, smiled and waved at Brian, then sat with his hands folded in his lap.

Brian smiled and waved back. He realized there was something he had to do.

Coach Channing was in a corner of the dugout, putting together the starting lineup. Brian walked over. "Coach," he said, "I'd like to ask you a favor."

"What's that, Brian?" He was only half listening.

"For today, I'd like you to start Adam Spinelli at short instead of me."

Coach Channing's head shot up. "Are you crazy? You're the best we've got. Adam—"

"Please, coach. Just for today. I've been working with Adam—"

"Well, all right. Are you feeling okay?"

Brian nodded, but when the lineup was posted, Adam came running over to him.

"What's going on? Why aren't you starting?"

"Because you are."

"But—"

"No buts. Go out and do it."

There was nothing more Adam could say, but as Andy took his warm-up pitches and the team fanned out into their positions on the field, Brian saw Mr. Spinelli smiling at his son. Sitting on the bench, Brian shouted, "Let's go, Rockets!"

67

And go they did. Andy came out smoking, and for the first two innings the Rams never had a chance. He walked one batter in the second, but the rest were ground balls and pop-ups.

Adam Spinelli had two chances at short. The first was a little pop-up that he squeezed neatly above his head. The second was a hard hit ground ball. He charged it, got it in his glove, then seemed to falter for a moment before letting go a perfect throw to first. As the ball smacked into Justin's mitt, Brian let out his breath.

At the plate the Rockets were doing well, too. Andy and Justin combined for a single and a double that scored a run, and after Pete Wyshansky walked and Jenny Carr singled, Michael Wong drove them both in with his first double of the year. Adam Spinelli flied out to short center field, but it didn't make any difference.

In the top of the third it was 3–0 Rockets. Still early in the game, but for some reason Andy came apart. The smoke turned into meatballs, and the Ram hitters jumped on three of them in a row, spraying singles all over the field and scoring a run. Luke and Coach Channing went out to settle Andy down, but when he walked the next batter to load the bases, the coach took him out—and brought in Brian!

Brian had been enjoying watching the game. He could see Andy was losing it and was not surprised when the coach asked him to warm up. He didn't expect to be called in with the bases loaded, though!

He took his warm-up pitches from the mound, got ready, checked the runners. Then he threw his best fastball, and the Ram hitter bounced it over third for a run-scoring single.

Three to two Rockets, and the bases were still loaded! Brian knew he had to pour it on. He worked the count on the next batter to one ball and two strikes, then struck him out on a change-up on the inside corner. The batter after that didn't have a chance. He got jammed on a fastball and popped up meekly to the mound.

The Rams never seriously threatened again. Brian scattered four hits over the next three innings, walked two, and didn't allow another run. Adam Spinelli made two more good plays at short and saved a run on a fine throw to the plate with two out in the fifth.

A good day in the field, but it was even better at the plate. Adam Spinelli drove in a run with a double down the left field line in the fourth. Brian drove in another with a triple to deep center in the fifth.

As he steamed into third and stamped on it, Brian heard cheers from the Rocket bench. *"Streak, streak, streak!"* he heard. *"Streak, streak, streak!"*

He raised his hands over his head, and as he did, he looked into the stands. There were his mom, Barbara, and Mickey, smiling and cheering for him!

Brian couldn't believe it. He grinned at them and waved, and when the game was over and won 5–2, he congratulated Adam and brought him along as he went to talk to Luke and Phil.

"I'm sorry I was such a jerk about the streak," Brian said. "I was really upset about my error, but I shouldn't have bragged like that."

He held out his hand. Luke shook it first, then Phil.

"Friends again?" said Brian.

"Friends again," said Luke, then Phil.

"Can we be friends with Adam, too?" Brian added. "He's a pretty good kid. Good ballplayer, too."

"Sure," said Luke.

"Sure," said Phil.

They both shook Adam's hand.

Looking over his shoulder, Brian said, "I think I have to go now."

He turned, and there were Mom, Barbara, and Mickey. They hugged him, and he hugged them back. As they walked away, they looked like a new family already.